REWIND

They see the things we can't see....

WATCHERS

#1 LAST STOP
#2 REWIND

WATCHERS

REWIND

PETER LERANGIS

AN
APPLE
PAPERBACK

SCHOLASTIC INC.
New York Toronto London Auckland Sydney
Mexico City New Delhi Hong Kong

ISBN 0-590-10997-9

12 11 10 9 8 7 6 5 4 3 2 1   8 9/9 9 0 1 2 3/0

Printed in the U.S.A.   40

First Scholastic printing, November 1998

For Bethany
With Countless Thanks

REWIND

WATCHERS
Case file: 6791

Name: Adam Sarno

Age: 14

First contact: 54.35.20

Acceptance:

They're gone.

It's time.

1

Adam felt cold. Cold and alone.

Darkness had swallowed the woods. His path was vanishing fast.

"Guys?"

The word died in the air, swept away by a shriek of north wind. Above him, branches waved wildly in the moonlight, clattering like old, brittle bones.

This was a stupid idea, Sarno.

He shouldn't have agreed to play laser tag. Especially here. Especially at this time of year, when the reminders were so strong.

He tried not to think of what had happened. It was four years ago. He had to get over it. He couldn't avoid the lake his whole life.

Thump.

Adam's heart nearly stopped.

"Ripley?" he called out. "Lianna?"

No answer.

Maybe they were hiding from him. Listening to his voice. Laughing at how it sounded. Timid. Scared. So very *Adam*.

(*Adam is a wimp . . .*)

Or maybe they'd left already. The lovebirds running off, not telling anyone.

Okay, fine.

No problem.

I know these woods.

I am ten blocks from home.

He slung his laser gun over his shoulder. To his right, the woods disappeared into blackness. To his left, the moon peeked through the trees, dimly lighting a path toward the lake. He could follow the trail along the bank to the big clearing, where his bike was.

No.

Stay away from the lake.

Adam ignored the thought. He was older now. Too old to be afraid.

It was only a memory.

Memories couldn't hurt you.

As he trudged to the lake, his heart began to race.

Warning signs were legible even in the faint moonlight: DANGER! THIN ICE! DO NOT ENTER UNDER PENALTY OF LAW!

Adam glanced beyond the signs. The lake looked remote. Unfriendly.

The last time he was on the lake, the signs didn't exist. You could sneak onto the ice and no one bothered you.

But the last time was four years ago. A January afternoon.

He did sneak onto the ice that day. To practice hockey.

Don't think about this now. Turn away.

But Adam's eyes fixed on a distant spot on the snow-dusted ice. In line with a clump of pine trees at the opposite bank.

That was where it had happened.

Lianna had been there. She had come along with —

Don't.

With Edgar.

Edgar didn't want to practice. I forced him.

They were ten. The hockey net was heavy, and no one was helping Adam set it up. Edgar was skating around, teasing Adam (*showing off for Lianna*), challenging him to take away the puck, being a total jerk, and (*I wanted to kill him*) that was it, wasn't it, that was the reason for the fight (*it's not my fault*), and when Edgar was pulled out of the hole, he had a big bump on his head (*because it hit the ice*), but Adam couldn't remember because he'd fallen in, too, and blacked out, and if it weren't for Lianna he would have died himself, which would have made more sense, because what did poor Edgar do to deserve what he got, a deadly blow to the head from his supposed best friend?

It's not my fault.

And the next thing Adam remembered, he was in the hospital, screaming (*Edgar! Edgar!*), while the doctors scratched their chins and told him it wasn't his fault (*they didn't see it, only Lianna did*), and from then

8

on, everything was different, he couldn't concentrate, and the kids at school steered clear
of him — but the rumors got back (*Adam
killed Edgar, whacked him in the head,
pushed him in the ice, and left him for dead*),
the rumors he ignored even though *they were
true, weren't they?*

Stop.

He began to run. Away from the lake.
Blindly. His laser pack and coat snagged on
brambles, but he didn't care. He had to get
away. He had to go home.

*But where's Edgar? I can't leave without
Edgar.*

The thoughts were following him. Taunting
him.

Edgar is dead.

Dead. Dead. Dead.

"Help!"

Adam stopped in his tracks.

The voice was coming from behind him.

Real. And loud. As if reaching across time.

"Adam, help!"

*It's Ripley's voice, you fool. Ripley, not
Edgar.*

Adam spun around.

"Adaaaaaaam!"

"Oh my god . . ." he murmured.

It *wasn't* over.

It was happening.

Again.

We've almost got him.

Unless he gets himself first.

2

"**I**'M COMING!"

Adam's feet were flying. He sprinted toward the lake, high-stepping over roots and rocks.

"Ripley! Where are you?"

"Die, suckah!"

The light hit him square in the eyes.

Footsteps. Someone was running up to him.

"Uh-oh. Are you okay?"

Adam blinked and looked up. "R-Ripley?"

Ripley Weller was standing over him. His

laser pack glowed dully on his chest. "What were you yelling about?"

"It's just that — I thought you were — you shouted for help —"

"Did you really think I was in trouble?" Ripley grinned, clasping his hands to his heart. "Oh, *Adam.* I didn't know you *cared.*"

He was alive. And well.

And still a jerk.

"FREEZE!"

Ripley's smile vanished. He clutched his gun and spun around.

Too late. A direct hit. Right to the center of his pack.

"Yyyyyyes!" Lianna Frazer emerged from the trees, pumping her fists in triumph. "The winner and new Vermont champion!"

"It was a time-out," Ripley said. "Adam was wounded."

"Yeah, right. I killed you!" Lianna turned to Adam. "You're my witness, Adam. Didn't I kill him?"

Kill him.

Adam's teeth were chattering. "I guess."

Ripley shot Adam a look of disgust.

"Thanks a lot. You *always* agree with her, Sarno."

"Only when I'm right," Lianna said.

"Lianna's own personal slave." Using two different simpering, high-pitched voices, Ripley chanted: " 'Nice day, Adam.' *'Yes, Lianna.'* 'Do my homework, Adam?' *'Okay, Lianna.'* 'Jump off a cliff for me?' *'Right away, Lianna.'* "

"Cram it, Weller." Lianna turned and walked away, glancing briefly at Adam.

Say something. Don't just stand there.

Words tumbled around in Adam's head. Defenses. Insults. But they were lame. Ripley would easily swat them aside.

"Not that I blame you, Adam," Ripley said with a smirk. "I mean, hey, if it weren't for her, you'd be a stiff at the bottom of the lake like what's-his-name."

Lianna spun around. *"Stiff?"*

"Corpse, whatever," Ripley replied uneasily.

"Never. Speak. About him. Like that. Again." With each word, Lianna advanced on Ripley, backing him up until he was trapped against a tree.

15

"It was a joke," Ripley protested.

Lianna pressed her face close to his. "Edgar died that day. He was Adam's best friend. You didn't live around here back then. You don't know what any of us went through. My advice to you is *watch your mouth.*"

"Fine." Nodding nervously, Ripley slipped away.

Adam forced his gaping jaw shut.

He'd never seen Lianna like this.

She defended me.

Brave Lianna rescues Adam the Wimp.

I will never, ever hear the end of this.

"Thanks," he muttered.

But Lianna wasn't paying attention to him. She was staring at the lake. In the reflected moonlight, Adam could see her face slacken. A slight change, something no one would notice. No one but Adam.

She was thinking about it.

The accident.

"It was four years ago Saturday," Adam said softly.

Lianna shot him a look.

"I know this is crazy," Adam continued,

"but when I heard Ripley yelling, I thought it was Edgar."

Lianna nodded and turned away. "Let's go, Adam. What's past is past."

She jogged off, her footfalls echoing in the cold, dry air.

Adam stole one last look at the lake.

That's all it was. A body of water.

The rest was just memory. Brain waves.

Nothing more.

Lianna was turning off the lake path now, onto the narrow trail that led toward the clearing.

Adam ran to catch up. But as he veered onto the trail, something yanked at his foot.

He stumbled to the ground. Wrapped around his ankle was the strap to a small backpack.

"Wait up!" he cried.

Adam pulled the strap away. The pack was small but heavy.

In a moment his two friends were running toward him.

"Eeek. Kill it before it multiplies!" Ripley speared his laser rifle through the straps, lifting the backpack off the ground.

"Leave it," Lianna said.

"No way," Ripley shot back. "Let's look for ID. Send it back to the owner."

"Anonymously, right? With just some of the valuables missing?" Lianna snatched the pack from his rifle.

"Give it back!" Ripley protested. "Finders keepers."

"Adam was the finder," Lianna reminded him.

"Oh, and he won't steal a *thing*, right?" Ripley said mockingly. "Because he's such a good boy."

Out.

It was time to get out of the woods. This argument was ridiculous. "Look, it doesn't matter to me. You take it, Ripley. I don't mind."

Lianna shoved the backpack into Adam's hands. *"Mind*, Adam," she said wearily. "Stand up for the right thing once in a while."

With that, she and Ripley headed for the clearing.

Clutching the backpack, Adam followed.

He felt about two feet tall.

He has it.

Let's hope he knows what to do with it.

3

Ripley's house.

Adam still had trouble calling it that.

The Wellers had lived there for three and a half years. They had replaced the windows. Built an extension. Widened the driveway and relandscaped the lawn.

But Adam saw the old things. The wall that Edgar and Adam had helped paint. Edgar's basketball hoop, still hanging on the garage. The outline of the name HALL on the mailbox where the letters had been removed.

To Adam, it was still Edgar's house.

Even now, as Ripley rode up the driveway, Adam imagined his old friend standing and waving good-bye.

Stop.

What's past is past.

He and Lianna waved back, then began to pedal away.

"Sorry I yelled at you before," Lianna said.

"Well, Ripley got it much worse than I did." Adam smiled. "I didn't realize you still had a temper."

"When he said that about Edgar, I freaked. Especially after what *you* said, about hearing Edgar's voice."

"It wasn't only hearing," Adam replied. "I thought I was *seeing* the accident. Like a flashback."

"Adam, that is weird."

"I still have nightmares, too. All the time. Strong ones, where everything is so clear."

Lianna looked at him. "Everything?"

No.

Not everything.

Edgar's teasing, yes. The angle of the sun and the smell of the air. The weight of the net. The incredible frustration at Edgar.

After that, the dream always became muddy. Fragmented.

Even the fight was a blur.

The fight that had started it all.

I was a hothead. I couldn't control myself back then.

"I can't remember the fight," Adam said, "or the accident."

Lianna exhaled. "You're lucky. I wish I could forget them."

After the accident, Lianna had told him what happened. She'd told the TV stations and newspapers, too. Adam had saved all the articles. Over the years, he'd read them a thousand times, trying to spark a memory. Trying to free what he'd blocked.

The ice broke. Edgar fell in. The crack spread toward me. I tried to run away, but I wasn't fast enough. Lianna reached for us both. Edgar was flailing and almost pulled her in. But I was still. Unconscious. So she pulled me out and ran to get help. The ambulance came and took Edgar and me to the hospital. By then, Edgar was already . . .

Lianna was looking at him with concern. "You don't still blame yourself, do you?"

23

"I shouldn't have been so mad at him," Adam replied.

"Adam, we all get mad. That doesn't make us murderers."

Don't ask her. Don't bring it up —

The words flew out of Adam's mouth. "Did I hit him, Lianna? Is that where the bump on his head came from?"

Lianna's face darkened. "That was a *rumor*, Adam. Forget it. It's not worth your time."

"What exactly did I do? Did I even *try* to save him — ?"

"Adam, please! You think it's easy for me to talk about this? Be *grateful* you don't remember."

She's not saying I didn't do it.

They were in front of Lianna's house now. She turned sharply up her driveway.

Adam squeezed his brakes and turned. His bike slipped out from under him. He put out his leg to stop a fall.

The backpack, which he'd hooked over his laser pack, slipped off his shoulder. It fell to the street.

Thud.

The sound was sharp, metallic.

Lianna turned. "Klutz," she said with a wry smile.

Before Adam could react, she glided over and lifted the pack off the street. Balancing it on her handlebars, she unzipped it and reached in.

She pulled out a small videocamera.

Great. It had to be something expensive.

"Don't fool with it," Adam said.

But Lianna was already flicking buttons. Peering through the viewfinder. The red indicator light beamed above the lens.

"No image," Lianna said, handing the camera back. "You busted it."

"The owner's going to sue me."

"He'll be happy someone found it." Lianna yawned. "Don't sweat it, Adam. You worry too much."

As she pedaled up her driveway, Adam lifted the viewfinder to his eye.

Now the camera was working. Sort of. It was glowing with a blurry image of the street.

He adjusted the focus. The image sharpened, but the street looked totally washed

25

out. The cars, trees, houses — everything was blanketed in white, as if it had snowed.

Maybe it can be repaired.

Adam dropped the videocamera in the backpack, put both packs around his shoulders, and set off down the street.

He'd deal with it tomorrow.

Did he see?

He must have.

Then why — ?

4

"Rise and shine!"

Dad.

Adam's eyes blinked open.

He was awake.

The last images of his dream still clung to his consciousness. *The* dream.

It had started the same as always. The walk to the lake. The net. The start of practice.

But this time, it hadn't gotten fuzzy. He had seen what happened to Edgar. And it wasn't the way he'd thought it had been. It was worse. Much worse.

Hold on to it. HOLD ON . . .

Too late.

Adam sat up, groggy and mush-mouthed. As he yawned, his head throbbed. The smell of fried eggs wafting up from the kitchen only made him feel worse.

As his eyes adjusted to the light, the sight of the backpack startled him, black and unfamiliar on his desk. Through an open zipper, the videocamera lens glinted dully at him. Watching.

Adam staggered to the desk. He removed the camera and set it down, facing the wall.

A thick, sealed manila envelope fell out from the backpack onto his desk. Adam picked it up and turned it over.

No address.

He examined the backpack for tags. Nothing.

He tilted the videocamera, hoping to see some ID on it.

Click.

The red indicator light blinked on.

Must have jolted it.

He held the camera up and peered through the viewfinder. The dark, shadowy confines of his closet filled the frame, along with a string of tiny glowing indicators Adam noticed 7:48 A.M. and January 13. Right on the nose.

"Adam?" his dad called from downstairs. "Are you up?"

"Coming!" He swung the videocamera around, sweeping it across his room.

His eyes focused on a chest of drawers in the corner — his old one, which his mom had thrown out last year. Or so she'd claimed.

He smiled.

When did she sneak that in here?

Adam lowered the camera.

The chest was gone.

"What the — ?"

Quickly he looked through the viewfinder again.

The chest was back.

He panned the camera around the room, slowly.

A paperback copy of *Mossflower* was on the bed. He hadn't seen it in ages.

A hockey uniform lay on the floor, identical to the one he'd worn the day of the accident.

A spiral notebook was next to it — marked ADAM SARNO, 5-208.

Grade 5. Room 208.

All my old stuff.

In my old room.

A dream. He had to be dreaming.

Adam set the camera down. He rubbed his eyes, then cast a long, level glance around the room.

Everything was normal. No dresser. No uniform.

He pinched himself. Hard enough to hurt.

Okay, you are officially awake. Do not freak. Look through the videocamera again. Everything will be normal. Then you can go eat breakfast.

He swallowed. Lifted. Looked.

"Adam, you're going to be late for school!" his dad's voice boomed out.

Adam opened his mouth to reply, but no sound came out.

My old pajamas . . . the Monopoly game, with the cover still intact . . . the radio I threw out last year . . .

WHAT IS GOING ON?

His eye shot down to the bottom of the frame. To the electronic indicators.

The correct time. The correct month and day.

But Adam stared at the last numeral. The year.

He clicked the RESET button. He tried to change the setting.

Nothing happened.

The YEAR setting was stuck.

Four years earlier.

He doesn't have much time.

Who?

Adam.

I thought you meant the other one.

Yes, him too.

5

Adam ran down the stairs two at a time. He darted past the kitchen.

Please please please let this be a figment of my imagination.

His mom and dad looked up curiously from the morning newspaper.

"Forgot to do some homework," Adam called out.

He went into the den, pulled a blank video-cassette from a shelf, and tucked it under his shirt.

If it's not a figment, I want proof.

He bounded back up to his room. Quickly he inserted the tape into the videocamera, pressed RECORD, and looked through the viewfinder.

Yes.

The old room filled the frame. The wrong year glowed on the indicator.

He would have it on tape.

Evidence.

"Homework?" his dad's voice thundered up from the kitchen. "Adam Sarno, I want an explanation now!"

Adam jumped.

"Coming!" He lowered the camera and set it on his desk. Then he ran for the door.

And the room blipped.

Not a flash of light, exactly. A flash of *something*. A momentary blur of colors. Along with an odd popping sound.

Adam stopped. He looked over his shoulder. The videocamera was angled slightly away from him, pointing to the center of the room. Still on.

Slowly he retraced his steps backward and sideways, closer to the camera's line of sight.

Blip.

The old hockey uniform materialized on the floor. Under his foot.

He choked back a gasp.

Slowly he lifted his eyes upward.

The videocamera had disappeared. Only the lens remained. It floated in the air, a hovering eye.

Under it was a mess of papers.

Fifth-grade homework.

The Monopoly game, *Mossflower*, the spiral notebook. It was all exactly as he'd seen through the lens.

But he wasn't looking through the lens anymore.

He was in front of it.

In the room.

In the past.

Trapped.

Panic raced through him. He had to get out.

The lens. Move away from it.

Adam darted to the left. Toward his door.

Blip.

The flash again. The shift in colors. The popping sound.

He was back. His room was exactly the way he'd left it. The old stuff was gone.

The videocamera was intact on his desk. Not just a floating lens.

And Adam's mind was racing.

Can I control this?

Can I go back and forth?

Am I nuts?

Before he could answer that last question, he stepped in front of the camera again.

Blip.

The flash and the popping noise no longer scared him.

As the past reassembled itself, Adam took a long, hard look around.

He noticed what he'd been too panicked to see before.

The colors, for instance. They were muted, a little too brown. The sounds — a passing car, the hissing of the upstairs shower — were dull, softened.

The light through the window was unusually bright. He looked out.

Snow.

He thought about what he'd seen through

the viewfinder last night, outside of Lianna's house. The bleached-out street.

The camera wasn't broken at all. I was seeing snow.

He thought back to four years ago. Had it snowed then? He couldn't remember.

Adam walked across the room. He ran his fingers over the bedsheets. He reached behind his headboard and felt the hardened lumps of chewed bubble gum he'd always put there.

Until Mom made me clean it all off. At age ten.

He turned toward his shelves and saw a book — *Time and Again* by Jack Finney, which he hadn't seen since he lent it to Lianna in seventh grade.

He reached for it.

His finger made contact. He could feel the texture of the binding as he pulled.

But the book barely budged.

It was as if it were made of some strange new substance — somehow solid but somehow not, a density of air.

He pulled harder. Really yanked. The book teetered toward him.

Thud-thud-thud-thud.

Adam spun around. Behind him, the book fell to the floor.

Dad was charging angrily up the stairs. Adam recognized the heavy footsteps.

But *which* Dad? Past or present?

Whatever. He was in the wrong place for either.

He leaped out of camera range.

Blip.

His room — his current, totally solid room — materialized around him.

Dad of the present charged in. His eyes shot right to the videocamera. "This is your homework?"

"Video class," Adam blurted out. "I mean, video *project*. Communication arts class."

"Where'd you get this?" He was heading for the camera now.

"No!" Adam rushed in front of him.

But it was too late.

Dad lifted the camera to his right eye.

And looked through.

Order a file on the father.

Not necessary.

Why?

Because only the boy can see.

6

"*It's broken.*"

All day long, Mr. Sarno's words stayed with Adam.

He didn't see it. Lianna didn't see it.

I'm the only one.

Which meant either the camera was defective, or Adam was crazy.

The tape would tell. He was dying to see it.

He kept the videocamera with him in school. It was in the old backpack, stuffed into the bottom of *his* pack. Now, as he pedaled away from school with Lianna and Ripley, he could feel it jabbing against his back.

"I hate surprises," Lianna remarked.

"You'll like this one," Adam said.

"It better be good," Ripley grumbled. "And quick. I have hockey practice."

They glided onto Locust Avenue and then swerved up Ripley's driveway. "Ripley," Adam said as he dropped his bike in the backyard, "it'll blow you away."

If it works.

Adam hadn't seriously thought about the alternative. But as he climbed the stairs to Ripley's room, he began shaking.

What if it doesn't?

Humiliation. His friends would know he was loony.

Stop. Think positive.

If it *did* work, if he'd captured the past on tape, if the camera *was* seeing what happened four years ago . . .

Saturday. Three o'clock.

The accident.

He would have to go there. Take the video-camera to the lake.

And see.

No. Don't even think about it.

It would happen again. Before his eyes. No more fragmented visions. No more blocked memories.

Cold, hard images.

He would know. For sure.

And that part scared him the most.

Ripley had to force his bedroom door open against a pile of old clothes. They slid into the room, sweeping puffballs of dust before them.

"How can you live like this?" Lianna asked.

Ripley picked up the pile and tossed it onto a wicker basket full of mud-encrusted football gear. "The butler's on vacation."

Her lips curled in disgust, Lianna sat on the edge of Ripley's bed.

Adam set his backpack next to her. He pulled out the other pack and placed it on the bed. The unmarked manila envelope peeked out of the open zipper. Taking out the video-camera, he ejected the tape.

Rrrrrrip. Lianna was tearing open the manila envelope.

"What are you doing?" Adam cried out.

"It might have ID." Lianna pulled out a

sheaf of newspaper clippings. "Oops. I'm sorry, Adam. Why didn't you tell me this stuff was yours?"

She held out the pile. From the top article, a headline jumped out at Adam.

TEN-YEAR-OLD EASTON BOY FALLS THROUGH ICE, DIES

Death Could Have Been Averted, Police Chief Says

Adam quickly paged through the others.

Inquest Rules Death an Accident . . . Suspicions of Foul Play Investigated . . . Easton Parents Demand Safety Referendum . . .

All clippings about Edgar's death.

Fresh clippings. With straight-cut edges, unyellowed by time. Police memos, hospital notes, detective reports — stuff Adam had never even seen before.

What on earth —?

"They're not mine," Adam said.

"Who else could they belong to?" Lianna asked.

"I don't know!" Adam replied.

"And why would anybody be carrying them around?"

Good question.

The camera, the clippings. The backpack.

Whose?

Why?

"Maybe the guy is a reporter. Or a cop." Ripley took an article from the top of the pile and began reading: " 'Ten-year-old Easton native Lianna Frazer was lauded by the Easton Chamber of Commerce for her heroism in response to a tragic accident in which horseplay during a hockey game led to the drowning of Edgar Hall, also ten. Her quick actions in summoning adult help were credited for saving the life of Alan Sarno. . .' Well, at least they got one name right."

"This is *too* weird," Adam muttered.

"Okay, simple explanation," Lianna said. "These belong to your parents. They fell off a shelf into the backpack."

Adam shook his head. "When I opened the backpack last night, this envelope was already in it. I saw it."

"You *thought* you saw a lot of things last night."

49

"You . . . are . . . being . . . followed," Ripley intoned dramatically, picking up the video-camera and pointing it at Adam. "Uh-oh. Bad news. The camera, she is broken."

"I could have told you that," Lianna said.

The camera. Think about the camera, Sarno. Worry about the clippings later.

"Actually, this is why I wanted to come here," Adam said, measuring his words. "See, the camera *isn't* broken."

"Look for yourself." Ripley held the camera to Adam's face.

Adam took it and looked through the view-finder.

Blue.

Blue wallpaper. Blue bedsheets and carpets. He was staring at an image of Edgar's room.

And then he saw Edgar.

His feet were propped up on his desk. He was fiddling with a handheld video game. Avoiding homework.

Oh my god.

He was alive.

Happy.

The indicator light read January 13. Edgar died on the fifteenth.

He had two days.

Warn him!

"Ed —" he blurted out.

Adam cut himself off.

This was insane. Edgar couldn't hear him.

As he put the camera down, Lianna and Ripley were both staring at him.

"Uh, Earth to Adam?" Ripley said.

"I — I saw —" Adam stammered.

Don't tell them. They won't believe it.

Let them see for themselves.

Show the tape.

Adam grabbed the tape from the bed and put it in Ripley's VCR. He rewound it and pressed PLAY.

The screen blinked to life.

A fuzzy image took shape. Bed. Dresser. Hockey uniform on the floor.

Yes.

YES!

"You *see*?" Adam blurted out.

"Adam, that's your old bedroom," Lianna said.

"*Exactly.* When I was ten." The view began to shift — just as Adam remembered it, moving around as he had moved the camera.

"This is what you wanted to show us?" Ripley said. "Your very first home video?"

"You didn't have a videocamera when you were ten, Adam," Lianna remarked.

"Right. I recorded what you're seeing with *this* camera. When I look through the lens, the camera sees the past. The place is right, the time and day are right — but it's all four years earlier."

"*Four years?*" Lianna gave him a sharp look.

She gets it.

"January thirteenth. Two days before Edgar died. Which means —"

"You expect me to believe this?" Lianna asked. "Why can't I see any of it? Why can't Ripley?"

"I don't know!" Adam replied.

Ripley reached for the remote. "This is ridiculous. I have to go —"

"Wait," Lianna said. "What's *that*?"

Something in the image was moving.

Not a solid object, really. More like a distor-

52

tion in the air, a shimmer in the shape of a human.

Adam's shape.

It passed into the frame on the right side, then out again.

The same path I took this morning when I started to go to breakfast. In and out of the past. The first time the room blipped.

The shape reappeared.

Yes. When I stepped back in. To look around.

It wandered across the frame, stopping at the window, reaching behind the headboard, trying to pull the book off the shelf . . .

Adam could barely breathe.

I am not insane.

The scene I saw was real. It's on tape.

And I was in it.

"Now, *that's* pretty cool," Ripley said. "How did you edit your image in like that?"

"That's me!" Adam protested. "I stepped in front of the lens, and I was in the image. In the past. Well, maybe not totally, physically. You saw the shape. Maybe just a part of me was there. My body aura or something."

Ripley nodded solemnly. "Or your body

odor. Sometimes that takes on a life of its own."

"Adam, you're scaring me," Lianna said.

"You don't believe me?" Adam asked.

Ripley burst out laughing. "I believe you are seriously, seriously ill."

From the TV, Adam heard a faint whistling. He turned to look.

The image was still. The angle was low, about waist level.

The camera was resting on the desk. I was downstairs, eating. I'd left it on.

Another figure was entering the frame.

This one was not a ghostly shimmer.

It was Adam. At age ten.

Me.

I'm watching me, not knowing I'm being watched.

Ripley narrowed his eyes. Lianna watched intently.

The younger Adam pulled the sheets up on his bed. Then he grabbed some books from his dresser and quickly stuffed them in a backpack.

As he was about to leave the frame, he stopped.

54

Leaning down, he picked up a book.

Even in the dim light, the title was visible.

Time and Again.

The ten-year-old Adam looked puzzled. Wondering how the book got there.

Only the fourteen-year-old Adam knew.

A tape. We should have planned for this.

He is resourceful.

But the girl — must not know.

Nor the boy.

Perhaps we should pull the project.

Give it time.

1

"Adam, this is creepy." Lianna paced the room.

I can convince her.

"I saw Edgar," Adam blurted out. "A few minutes ago, when I looked through the lens."

Lianna blanched. "But you *couldn't*. Edgar is dead."

"Not four years ago. Not yet."

Ripley glared at him in disbelief. "You superimposed images over an old cassette."

"Then how did the *image* move that book?" Adam asked.

"Coincidence," Ripley said. "It fell."

"I pulled it down!" Adam insisted.

Ripley grabbed the camera and thrust it toward Adam. "Okay, time traveler. You have special powers? Prove it."

Adam's fingers closed around the videocamera. He looked for a place to set it down.

No.

You'll be in the same room as Edgar.

Inches from him.

Knowing he's about to be killed.

And you won't be able to do a thing.

"I can't," Adam said. "Not here."

"I thought so," Ripley said with a grin. "Okay, guys, we've had our fun. I have hockey practice in ten minutes."

"Adam?" Lianna said. "Was this all some kind of joke?"

She was glaring at Adam. Disappointment, accusation, betrayal, and fear all passed across her eyes.

He was losing her.

His only possible partner.

Do it, Sarno.

Stand up for the right thing once in a while.

He slid a pile of papers to the back of Ripley's desk and set the camera down. "Okay. I changed my mind."

He turned the camera on.

Lianna's eyes fixed on him.

Ripley yawned.

Slowly Adam stepped in front of the lens.

"I still seeeeee you . . ." Ripley taunted.

Blip.

Adam felt a momentary pull. A smear of color, the *pop* . . .

And then, blue.

Edgar's blue.

Adam was facing Edgar's mirror. It showed an empty room.

No reflection. As if I'm not here.

He moved closer.

And he saw the room wasn't empty.

Edgar was behind him to the left. Still sitting at his desk. Writing. His back to Adam.

It hurt to see him. Worse than Adam expected. He felt it sharply in his gut as he turned around.

He wanted to yell out. Warn him.

But Adam was a phantom. A ghost. Invisible and silent.

How can you be sure?

Try it.

"Edgar?" Adam walked closer, his voice little more than a whisper.

Edgar didn't turn around. He was writing intently.

Adam looked over his shoulder. Edgar was recording hockey statistics. Goals and assists for each player. Game by game.

Several columns were full of numbers. The right side was blank — the upcoming games, beginning January 16.

Games Edgar would never play.

Reach him.

Adam lifted his hand. He placed it on Edgar's shoulder.

He could feel the fabric. Barely.

But Edgar wasn't reacting.

REACH HIM!

Adam tried again. As if the touch would pull Edgar away from the lake. As if it would shield him, protect him from death.

Edgar dropped his pen.

With a flick of the wrist, he swatted his shoulder. Right where Adam had touched it.

Blip.

The surroundings melted into a brief swirl of blue.

Ripley's room instantly materialized around him.

Ripley was holding the camera. The red light was off. "Enough," he said.

What are you doing?" Adam pleaded.

"Not Oscar material," Ripley remarked. "I'd say C plus for the hysterical emotions, but A minus for the pantomime."

"Pantomime? But Edgar was — couldn't you see?"

"Adam," Lianna said, "you were here the whole time, doing all these strange gestures."

This is not happening.

Adam took the camera out of Ripley's hands, set it back on the desk, and turned it on. "Go. Somebody try it besides me!"

Ripley grinned. "Escape into the past!" he cried, grabbing Lianna by the waist.

"Ripley, *no!*" Lianna screamed.

But it was too late.

They were both standing in front of the lens now.

Lianna was sweating, glancing around uncertainly.

A look of wonder passed across Ripley's face.

He sees it!

"Can you hear me?" Adam called out. "What do you see?"

"Oh, wow . . ." Ripley said. "There's Washington crossing the Delaware . . . Lincoln emancipating the slaves . . . *Leave It to Beaver* making its season premiere . . ."

Lianna rolled her eyes. "Ripley, you're a jerk."

PROGRESS REPORT

Subject: Adam Sarno

ACCEPTANCE SUBMENU

Phase 1. <u>Discovery</u>.   PASSED.

Phase 2. <u>Facility</u>.   PASSED.

Phase 3. <u>Commitment</u>.   PASSED.

Phase 4. <u>Fulfillment</u>.

8

Edgar felt my touch.

Adam bounded down Ripley's back stairs and lifted his bike upright off the grass.

"So I can take it?" Ripley asked.

Adam heard the words, but they weren't registering.

Which means I can do something. I can affect the past.

"HELLO?" Ripley shouted. "ARE YOU HEARING ME, ADAM?"

"Huh?" Adam said.

"Read my lips," Ripley said. "Can I take your videocamera? To try to fix it?"

Adam slung the backpack around his shoulder. "It's not broken."

And it may help me save a life.

Somehow.

If he could make his presence felt, maybe he *could* warn Edgar. Prevent him from going to the lake.

Lianna was riding her bike in slow circles on the driveway, lost in thought.

"Oh, you have plans?" Ripley asked. "Maybe a trip to ancient Greece tonight?"

"Stop it, Ripley!" Lianna spoke up. "You just want to figure out how *you* can travel into the past."

Ripley's jaw dropped. "Whaaaat?"

"Maybe he sees something we don't," Lianna said. "And you can't deal with it."

"Whoa, Lianna, you've been hanging around the Time Nerd too long. Come with me to practice. Slap a few. Come to your senses."

Lianna glowered at him. "You know I hate hockey."

She did. Even back then. Edgar dragged

her to practice that day. He had such a crush on her.

"Suit yourself." Ripley's jaw was clenched. "Enjoy your delusions. Both of you."

Ripley hopped on his bike and rode away. Lianna and Adam went in the other direction.

For a long time neither spoke. Finally Adam said, "You do believe me, don't you?"

"I want to," Lianna replied. "But how can it be true? How do I know you're not playing a prank on Ripley?"

"I don't *know* how to play a prank, Lianna. Look, you have to be on my side. You know what this means. We can *do* something about the accident. Change it."

They came to a stop in front of the Frazers' house. Lianna gave Adam a hard, appraising look. "Okay, Sarno, I want you to take out the camera, look at my house, and tell me what you see. Right now."

Adam did as he was told. He trained the videocamera on Lianna's front porch. "The yard is full of snow," he reported. "There's a snow creature in front — looks like a dinosaur. Let's see . . . a car's pulling up the driveway, a dark blue Chevy, license plate

69

908-EZN. An old lady's getting out . . . I think it's your grandmother . . . and Jazz is running out the front door to greet her."

Jazz.

Adam smiled sadly. Jazz had died around the same time as Edgar did. Adam never knew how it happened. At the time, other things were on his mind.

Lianna's face was drawn. "I remember that visit. It was the last time Grandma drove a car. As she was leaving, she put the car in the wrong gear and ran over Jazz."

"I didn't know . . ."

"I was so upset, I didn't tell anyone. And Edgar's accident happened the next day. It was the worst week of my life. Grandma was so freaked about what happened to Jazz, she gave up driving."

And eventually she died, too.

A train accident. About two years ago. Adam remembered it vaguely.

"That's why she started visiting us by train . . ." Lianna's voice trailed off.

"I'm sorry." He put an arm tentatively around Lianna's shoulder.

She leaned into him and said softly, "I believe you, Adam. About the camera."

Finally.

Adam smiled. "Lianna . . . I'm going to *use* this thing . . . to save Edgar."

"How?"

"I'm not sure. I can move things in the past. I can make myself be felt. Maybe I can warn him. Or push him away."

"But that's impossible. You can't change the past."

"Maybe. Maybe not. No one's ever tried it."

"Wait a minute." Lianna shook her head. "Edgar died, Adam. It's a fact. He's not here. So even if you go to the lake on Saturday and do all you can, it won't work. It can't. Because if it could, he'd be with us today."

"Just because Edgar's not around, it doesn't mean I never saved him. I just haven't saved him *yet*. Saturday hasn't come."

Lianna sighed. "Look, Adam. Maybe you do see the past. Maybe you even travel into it, in some form. But don't delude yourself. What's done is done. Try this, and you'll just end up watching the accident all over again."

"Maybe. But that's all right, too. At least I'll finally know exactly what happened."

"You already *do*. How is it going to feel to stand there and watch your best friend die — again? Do you really want that?"

No. I don't.

Just being in Edgar's room was painful enough.

This might be too much too bear.

But if I don't, I'll lose my chance forever. I'll never know.

And that would be worse.

"I'm not sure," Adam said. "Maybe you could come with me."

Lianna looked horrified. *"Are you out of your mind?* I will not go through that again."

"But you won't see it. Only I will."

"I'll be *experiencing* it through you. And I'll have to pick up the pieces when you totally freak out."

"I guess I never thought of it that way."

"Well, *think* for a change, Adam. It's a stupid idea. Totally stupid. Take my advice. Forget you even thought of it."

With that, she turned and rode up her driveway.

This is what I feared.

9

"For homework, you may begin the unit on secants . . ."

Adam had no idea what his math teacher was saying. He was exhausted. He hadn't slept at all last night.

He looked at the wall clock. Almost 3:00.

Twenty-six more hours.

He fingered a crumpled-up note, opening it inside his math textbook.

A-

I'm sorry for yelling at you.

Meet me after school in the lobby.

-L

All night long, he'd thought about what Lianna said. Bounced it back and forth.

He hadn't seen that look in her eye since . . .

The accident.

When the bell rang, Adam was the first out of the class.

The hallways were a jumble of noise and light. His head hurt. The backpack was weighing him down. He couldn't concentrate.

"Hey, cutie."

Adam had to do a double take. It was Lianna, but it didn't sound like her.

"Don't take it too personally," she said with a laugh. "I say that to all the boys."

Adam tried to return her smile confidently, nonchalantly. But he felt like an idiot.

Lianna's face grew serious. "I'm sorry about last night. I totally understand how you feel."

"Same here," Adam said. "I couldn't sleep thinking about this. I don't know what to do."

"Maybe this isn't the place to talk about it in detail. Come to my house after dinner — like, seven o'clock? We can watch a movie and talk."

"Sure," Adam said.

Over Lianna's shoulder, Ripley was approaching. He gave Adam a tight smile and put his arm around Lianna. "My house?"

Lianna looked at Adam. "We'd love to."

"We?" Ripley asked.

"Should we tell him, Adam?" Lianna asked.

Adam cringed.

Wrong, wrong question.

"Tell me what?" Ripley said.

"Nothing," Adam said feebly. "Uh, I have to go home."

"It's Friday. There's no homework," Ripley snapped. "What *kind* of nothing?"

Lianna shrugged. "You wouldn't believe it anyway."

"Try me."

Lianna looked helpless. And Ripley was not going to give up.

Adam sighed.

He knows what's up. I pulled him into this.

As they walked out to the bike rack, Adam began to explain his plan.

Ripley laughed at first. On the ride to his house, he fired some suspicious questions. But Adam kept at it. Patiently, matter-of-factly.

By the time they reached the Wellers' house, Ripley had fallen silent.

His sister, Caryn, was eating a snack in the kitchen as they trudged through.

"Don't say hi," she grumbled.

"Sorry," Ripley said absently.

An apology. Caryn looked stunned.

I have him. I think.

For what it's worth.

Ripley led Adam and Lianna up to his room. He shut the door behind them.

"Adam, this is risky," he said, pacing the floor.

"So you believe me?" Adam asked.

Ripley didn't answer for a long time. "I still need to see some evidence. More than that tape. What if I come with you Saturday?"

"What?" Lianna exclaimed. "You just said it was risky."

"Risky to do it *alone*," Ripley replied. *"You* don't want to go. I could be there to help, in case something goes wrong."

"I am not hearing this," Lianna said. "I don't know what's harder to believe — Adam's time travel or your conversion into a kind person."

Adam watched Ripley's face. Ripley was lost in thought, growing excited.

This was not a trick. It couldn't be.

"In the meantime," Ripley announced, "I'll try to fix the camera."

"So *that's* it!" Lianna said. "Ripley, the camera only works for Adam."

"It's got to be an eyesight thing," Ripley said. "You know, like some people can see certain frequencies that others can't."

"Frequencies?" Lianna repeated.

"Well, why do *you* think Adam's the only one? His inner specialness?"

"Ripley, you are missing the whole point!"

Ripley wheeled around to her. "But of course *you're* not," he said sardonically. "You *never* do!"

Enough.

Adam should have known Ripley had an ulterior motive.

He did not want to be in the room another minute. "I'll . . . get some snacks."

He slipped downstairs to the kitchen.

Caryn looked up from a magazine. "They fighting again?"

"I guess."

"Might as well go home. You don't want to be here when the fireworks start. It can get ugly."

Adam took a bag of pretzels from the cupboard and joined her at the table. He couldn't leave without his camera. He'd just have to wait it out.

Which, fortunately, didn't take long. When the sounds of arguing stopped, Adam headed back upstairs with the pretzels.

Ripley's door was closed. From behind it, Adam could hear low, urgent whispering.

He knocked.

Total silence.

Then Lianna called out, "Adam?"

Adam pushed the door open. Lianna and Ripley were sitting casually on the floor.

Too casually.

Adam looked over to where he'd set down his backpack.

The pack was there. Open and empty.

"Where's my videocamera?" Adam demanded.

Ripley reached down and pulled it out from a pile of clothes on the floor. "Here."

"What's it doing out of the bag?"

"We were just looking at it."

Adam grabbed the camera, turned it on, and looked through the viewfinder.

Edgar's room came into focus. Adam sighed with relief.

Then he spotted Edgar, off to the left, laughing hysterically. His mom was sitting on the windowsill, also laughing.

Mrs. Hall.

Adam felt a tug in his chest. He missed her, too.

He remembered what she looked like after Edgar's death. Gray. Haggard. As if she'd never smile again.

And now here she was, content. Young-looking. Full of beauty and hope. Not suspecting a thing.

She and Edgar were both looking at something off to the left, something that was making them laugh. Adam swung the camera around to see what it was.

"Adam?" Lianna said.

But Adam wasn't paying attention to her.

He saw a boy dancing around in a baggy Santa Claus suit with the hat pulled down over his head — the outfit Edgar's dad used to wear at the department store during Christmas.

The boy took off his hat and bowed.

It was Adam. Age ten.

Shaking, Adam put down the camera.

"What?" Lianna asked.

"Nothing," Adam replied. "I just saw me, that's all."

"Whoa," Ripley said. "This is, like, *so X-Files*."

Memories of that day were seeping into his brain — the Santa costume, followed by an evening of sledding in the moonlight.

He smiled.

He felt like crying.

Everything would be so much better if he were alive.

"I — I have to go," Adam said. "Ride around or something."

"I'll hold on to the camera for you," Ripley volunteered.

Lianna gave him a suspicious glance. "*I* will. Don't worry, Adam. I'll kill him if he touches it."

"No, thanks." Adam dropped the camera into the backpack.

"Really, it's no problem," Lianna said. "I can give it back to you tonight."

Ripley's face fell. "*Tonight?* You two have plans?"

Adam bolted before another argument could start.

That evening, Adam barely touched his dinner.

"Are you feeling all right?" Mrs. Sarno asked.

"Fine," Adam lied.

"Something's wrong if you're leaving food on the plate," his dad said with a concerned smile.

Adam pushed around his mashed potatoes with a fork. "When Edgar died, how did his parents take it?"

Mr. and Mrs. Sarno exchanged a glance.

"They were devastated, naturally," Mr. Sarno replied. "Why?"

"That must be *the* worst thing — losing your child," Adam said. "You'd probably give up everything in the world to get him back, wouldn't you?"

"Get him back?" Adam's dad said warily.

"I mean, what if I died? And what if someone told you it was possible to change the past? To go back and prevent that death from happening —"

"Adam, please," Mrs. Sarno interrupted.

"Just tell me! What if all that happened, Mom? And even though logically it made no sense, even though you might be risking your life if you followed through, you believed — you really believed — this crazy idea had a chance. Would you do it?"

"Frankly, Adam, I couldn't allow myself to imagine it," Mrs. Sarno said. "Can we change the subject?"

"Then pretend you're Mrs. Hall. *Would you?*"

Mrs. Sarno looked uncomfortably at her husband. "Yes," she said. "I suppose in her situation, hypothetically, I would."

"I wouldn't," Mr. Sarno said. "As painful as it would seem. You can never bring back what you've lost. It's the natural order of things."

Adam nodded.

His heart told him his mom was right.

His mind told him his dad was right.

He had to choose one.

Twenty hours.

10

Adam said he'd be at Lianna's by 7:00.
And it was already 6:50.

He took a deep breath and looked out his
bedroom window, toward the Frazers' house.

Their front door opened. Lianna emerged,
frowning. Arms folded, she paced across her
porch.

She's mad at me.

No. He wasn't late yet. It was something
else.

*She's just had a fight with Ripley. She's
dumping him.*

Because of me.

Adam felt a rush.

He was happy. Exhilarated.

Forget it. Don't even think about it.

He could not allow himself to be distracted. Lianna was a friend. Nothing else.

Besides, girls like her didn't go out with guys like Adam.

He pulled himself away from the window. The videocamera was sitting on his bed. He picked it up, trying to decide whether or not to take it.

Outside, a little dog was yapping loudly — Stetson, the mutt that belonged to Lianna's next-door neighbors. Adam watched him scamper onto the Frazers' porch, leaping onto Lianna's leg.

Adam smiled. Stetson looked a lot like Jazz.

Jazz. Who died the night before Edgar did.

Tonight. Adam lifted the videocamera to his eye. He trained it on Lianna's house.

The street was no longer a streak of dry blacktop.

It was snow-covered, just as it had been four years ago. A melted snow dinosaur stood on the lawn. The snowplows had been through, piling the drifts high against the curb. But Lianna's driveway had been dug out, and a dark blue Chevy was parked in it.

Adam could see the entire Frazer family silhouetted in the living room lights — the ten-year-old Lianna, her parents, her brother, and someone else . . .

The front door opened. Jazz came scampering out first, followed by the others.

Under the porch light, Adam could see a shock of white hair.

Lianna's grandma.

She was heading for her car.

Jazz was jumping up, placing his paws on her coat. Grandma petted him.

She's going to kill him.

Adam looked up. Into the present. Lianna had returned into the house. The street was empty.

He grabbed the camera, bolted from his room, and raced outside.

As he ran toward Lianna's, he raised the camera. The rubber flap of the viewfinder pounded into his eye socket.

His feet pounded dry pavement — even

though the image was snowbound, his body was *behind* the lens. In the present.

Grandma was in the car, waving out the window. The exhaust pipe belched smoke.

Clunk. The car shuddered as she put it in gear. She looked over her right shoulder.

Mr. Frazer shooed Jazz away from the back of the car. Yapping wildly, the little dog ran to the front.

"NO!" Adam yelled. Uselessly.

The car lurched forward.

Still holding the camera to his eye, Adam ran toward Jazz. He reached his other hand forward.

STOP HIM!

His hand was in the frame now. Adam could see its faint shimmer.

He felt Jazz's fur.

He shoved as hard as he could.

The motion threw him off balance. The camera went flying.

And Adam fell in front of the car.

11

He was pinned to the driveway. Under the car.

I'm dead. I tried to save two people and now I'm dead.

"Adam! What are you doing?"

Lianna's voice. Coming from the direction of the house.

In the sudden silence, he noticed the car was not moving. The engine was off.

He slid out from underneath. No snow on the ground.

Back.

In the present.

His head was throbbing. As he caught his breath, he noticed the car in the driveway. A newish green Volvo.

He didn't remember seeing it when he was looking out his window a moment ago, without the camera.

How could I have missed it?

It didn't matter. The videocamera was lying in the driveway. Dented. He scrambled toward it and quickly looked through the viewfinder.

The past glowed back at him.

Snow. The blue Chevy. Mr. and Mrs. Frazer at the driver's side, talking with Grandma heatedly.

"Adam?" Lianna was standing before him now. "Are you okay?"

Adam lowered the camera. "It didn't work."

"What didn't?"

"I went into the past and tried to change it."

"After all we talked about?" Lianna was angry.

Adam examined the camera. "I don't get it. *Something* should have happened."

"But nothing did, huh? I was right, wasn't I?"

"I thought I pushed him."

"Who?"

Look at the tape. See what went wrong.

Adam pressed the EJECT button.

The bay whirred open. But it was empty.

"What happened to the tape?" Adam asked.

"You left it at Ripley's," Lianna reminded him. "Now come inside. Your head is all banged up. And you're late for dessert and movies."

Adam slouched into the house after her.

Forget about helping Edgar.

All you can do is watch.

Watch the dead die again.

As Adam stepped into the living room, a blur of red-brown streaked toward him.

He staggered back.

He felt the weight of two small feet pressing into his thighs.

"Down, boy!" Lianna commanded. *"Jazz, leave him alone!"*

He did it.

Two new files have popped up ACTIVE.

Two?

One of them is the dog's.

12

I did it.

The dog was all over him. Licking him. Yapping excitedly.

It was shaggier than the dog Adam had just seen in the viewfinder. Older.

But definitely alive.

Lianna pulled Jazz away. "I don't know why he always does this to you, Adam. He just loves you so-o-o much."

"But — but — this is — *how can you be so calm?*" Adam stammered.

He knelt down and hugged the cocker

spaniel. He felt the warmth of Jazz's tongue on his cheek.

"Liannaaaaa!" a voice called from the kitchen. *"Is your boyfriend here yet?"*

"Yes!" Lianna called back. She smiled at Adam. "Sorry. That's what she says about any male."

Adam nodded. But he wasn't listening. He was staring at the white-haired woman in the kitchen entryway.

Lianna's grandmother.

"Oh . . . my . . . god," he murmured.

"I know." Lianna nodded, sniffing deeply. "Those cookies smell awesome. Let's go before Sam eats them all."

But she died in the train wreck.

I didn't save her — *just Jazz.*

Adam felt light-headed as he walked to the kitchen.

Mr. and Mrs. Frazer were bustling around, doing chores. Grandma was taking a tin of hot cookies to the table. Sam was reaching over her shoulder for an early helping.

Lianna sneered at her brother. "Pig."

"Swallow, please," Mrs. Frazer said.

Adam sat numbly. Grandma was approaching the table again with a tray of steaming mugs. "Here's your hot chocolate, Adam. *With* mini-marshmallows, just the way you like it."

How does she know that?

Adam tried to recall memories of Grandma, but he didn't have many. A couple of hand-shakes and some small talk, that was it.

It doesn't matter.

Everything's different now. I saved Jazz, and everything's different.

He suddenly thought about the car in the driveway.

"Uh, Mrs. Frazer . . ." he began tentatively. "Your Chevy . . . what ever happened to it?"

"I sold that hunk of junk, oh, three or four years ago," Grandma said. "The gears kept slipping."

"She almost ran over Jazz," Sam piped up.

Grandma sighed sadly. "Poor little puppy. I went into Drive instead of Reverse, and he was in front of the car."

"I never saw a dog jump so far," Mr. Frazer said.

Adam nearly choked on a marshmallow.

"I like my Volvo much better," Grandma said. "It makes me feel like a teenager."

"You drive like one," Sam commented.

"Sam!" Lianna said.

"The car's all dented up," Sam explained. "Dad says Grandma should give up driving."

"Oh?" Grandma said.

Lianna's dad and mom exchanged an apprehensive glance. "All I meant," Mr. Frazer said gently, "was that you might . . . *consider* giving up driving. Your eyesight —"

Grandma gave a little derisive hoot. "My eyes are holding steady, thank you very much."

She still drives.

She never killed Jazz, so she never gave up driving. And because she didn't give up driving, she never took that train . . .

It was all becoming clear.

Saving Jazz had saved Grandma.

Adam downed his hot chocolate in one gulp and stood up. "Thanks for the dessert. Lianna? Can we see that movie now?"

"Sure."

Taking his videocamera, he went into the den.

He let Lianna in and shut the door tightly.

"I don't believe this," he said. "I am spinning. *Do you realize what this means?*"

Lianna glanced at him curiously. "What *what* means?"

"Grandma. Jazz. *They're alive.*"

"Why shouldn't they be?"

Her eyes were blank. Baffled.

She doesn't know.

"Lianna, you know about the videocamera, right? About what it can do?"

"Adam, of course I do. That's why we're here. To talk about Ripley's ridiculous idea. It's bad enough *you* want to go. How can you possibly let him? And what on earth do you mean by —"

"I have to go. Because I *can* change the past, Lianna. I just did it. I saved Jazz's life — and your grandmother's."

"Uh . . . say that again?"

"Lianna, listen to me. As of a few minutes ago, you had no Grandma and no Jazz. Do you remember that?"

Lianna shrank back. "Adam, something has happened to you. You're crazy."

"Okay. How about the big train derailment

103

about two years ago — it killed about twenty people?"

"What's that got to do with —"

"Your grandmother was supposed to be on that train. Why? Because she was supposed to have given up driving. Why? Because exactly four years ago, on that day when her Chevy slipped into Drive, she ran over Jazz. She *killed* him. *But I changed that, Lianna!*"

Lianna reached for the doorknob, but Adam placed himself in her way.

"Let me go, Adam."

"Don't you see? I went into the past. I knew what was going to happen to Jazz, and I stopped it from happening. And now the whole past has just . . . reshuffled. As if the accident never happened."

"Please. Go home before I scream!"

"Don't. Think about it, Lianna! Didn't you say I couldn't change the past, because what's done is done?"

"Yes."

"Well, what if I *can*? What if I *did*? What if Jazz and Grandma really were dead, and I saved them? *What's done is done*, right?

104

Their deaths suddenly never happened — so you have no memory of it!"

"Nothing happened to them!"

"So that proves it!"

"Just because you say so? Just because you claim Grandma and Jazz died, I'm supposed to accept that? Adam, you could say that up until ten minutes ago, we were all chimpanzees — but zoom, you went into the past, changed that, and wiped out all memories."

Hopeless.

How could she believe him? How could anyone believe a story like this?

I *wouldn't believe it.*

He flopped down onto the sofa.

"And what about *your* memory?" Lianna asked. "Wouldn't it be wiped out, too, if what you say is true? Why do *you* remember these deaths?"

"I don't know! Maybe it's because I *did* the time travel. I *saw* both versions. I mean, I'm the same person. Even if I jump back and forth in time, my memory stays in a straight line. It records everything I see."

"That is the most horrible, ridiculous thing I've ever heard," Lianna said.

Stupid. Stupid. Stupid. If only I'd had a tape in the camera!

Adam spotted a package of blank videotapes in the Frazers' wall unit. He stood up and took one. "The next time I go into the past," he said, "I'll have proof."

He pressed EJECT and shoved the tape into the slot.

It stopped halfway.

He pushed harder. No luck.

"What the — ?" Adam peered into the tape bay. Bits of plastic and metal were twisted off, mangled. "It's broken."

"You dropped it pretty hard on the driveway."

"That wouldn't damage it on the inside, would it?"

Maybe . . . or maybe it's something else.

Adam thought back. He'd had the camera with him all day. No one could have tinkered with it.

Except for one time.

"Lianna, when I left Ripley's bedroom to get snacks, what did he do?"

"Are you suggesting . . .?" Lianna's voice trailed off. "Well, I did go to the bathroom for a minute. But Ripley wouldn't have done something like *that*."

"You said he wants to time travel. Maybe he tried to rig this for himself."

"You think so?"

Adam's head was throbbing. He stretched out on the sofa and took a few deep breaths.

Okay. Think.

You don't really need that tape.

The camera will work without it. It did for Jazz.

Just don't let Ripley near the camera before tomorrow.

"Sometimes I don't know what I see in him," Lianna said quietly. She began running her fingers through Adam's hair. "I mean, we're still together and all, but each day we seem farther apart."

Adam felt a sudden rush of feeling. And exhaustion.

His eyes were beginning to close.

"Go ahead," Lianna whispered. "Sleep."

She put a movie in the VCR. A dreamy, sappy soundtrack began to play.

Adam drifted off in a cloud of thoughts — Ripley, Lianna, Edgar, and a thousand other people all swirling around to the music of Lianna's video.

Then, once again, the accident began to assemble itself in a dream. Once again, he saw the ice and the swirl of hockey uniforms.

But the perspective was different. The dream was framed as if Adam were watching the past through the videocamera lens.

And just as the event unfolded, just as Edgar began skating around the younger Adam, taunting and teasing, Adam felt a tug. As if someone had entered the dream and was trying to take away his camera.

Ripley. It must be Ripley.

Adam's eyes opened.

Lianna was slowly pulling the videocamera out of his arms.

"What are you doing?" Adam cried out.

Lianna recoiled, letting go of the videocamera. "Nothing!"

"You're taking it!"

"I am *not*! How could you even *think* that? I just wanted you to be comfortable."

Easy. Take it easy.

"Sorry," Adam muttered.

"Adam, you are paranoid."

"I know. It's just — I had this dream — I was watching the accident — Ripley was taking my camera away."

"Adam, trust me. He will not get that camera. No way. No matter what he tells me to do — "

Lianna's face suddenly froze.

Adam's sleep-addled mind snapped to full attention. "What has he told you to do?"

"Nothing."

"Did he tell you to take the camera?"

"It doesn't matter, Adam. I have a mind of my own."

Adam felt a chill. He took the camera and stood up. "I better get home. Sorry, Lianna. I guess I *am* paranoid — and nervous."

Lianna shrugged and turned back to the TV. "I'll let you know how the movie ends."

Adam felt weak as he walked home.

He glanced backward at Grandma's car.

Was it there earlier?

He couldn't remember.

Maybe the whole episode was all some kind of concoction. Maybe Grandma and Jazz never died.

After the accident, the doctors had told him he'd had a concussion. Concussions were serious. You may forget things, they'd said. You may see things that haven't occurred.

And it may not happen right away. It may happen much later, when you least expect it.

Four years later?

Was that what was happening?

Maybe the camera was one big illusion.

Maybe I'm totally cracking up.

No. Not now.

13

*Z*ing.

Adam sprang out of bed.

He'd fallen asleep.

The videocamera was beside his bed.

Think.

Clear your head.

Okay, maybe this was some kind of vision. A concussion side effect.

But too many questions remained.

Why do I have no memory of Jazz or Grandma over the last four years?

How did that image of my old room get on the tape?

He couldn't afford to doubt.

He had to try.

He had to plan.

What if the rescue failed? What if three o'clock came and went and Edgar was still dead?

That would be it. No adjusting the camera. No turning back again.

It'll be like killing him twice.

Could he do something beforehand — keep him away?

He flicked on his desk lamp.

His clock showed 10:07 P.M.

Seventeen hours.

THINK!

Edgar's room.

No. It was Ripley's. Adam couldn't pop over there at this hour. Ripley would steal the camera.

Edgar's not the only one I can warn.

Adam reached for the videocamera. He turned it on and looked through the view-finder, scanning the room.

There. At his desk.

His younger self sat, fidgeting, absorbed in a computer game.

Adam put down the camera quickly and began scribbling on a pad of paper. He threw away several drafts until he got the note just right:

Hi. I know this sounds weird to you, but please trust this message — DO NOT GO TO THE LAKE TOMORROW UNDER ANY CIRCUMSTANCES. The ice is TOO THIN.

from, someone who cares

"There," Adam murmured.

All he had to do was leave it — unobtrusively, hidden in plain sight where his younger self would find it.

No ghostly confrontations, no shock.

Simple.

Adam's arms trembled as he picked up the camera.

Steady.

He focused again on his ten-year-old self.

Slowly he moved his hand into camera range.

Both hand and note shimmered, airy outlines in the old room. He dropped the note.

He pulled the camera away.

But the note was on *his* floor, in the present.

Adam picked up the note. He looked through the camera again and held the note in the viewfinder's range. Carefully he moved toward the bed and placed the note prominently on the old bedcover.

Again, he pulled the camera away.

The note was on his bed, as if the past didn't exist. As if the whole thing was —

No.

Do. Not. Doubt.

The rules. There had to be rules for time travel.

I can't bring anything into the past.

Maybe this was Rule Number One. It made weird sense.

Warning was out.

Rescuing was in. He'd proved that. Two lives saved. Nothing sacrificed.

Adam froze.

This is nothing like Jazz's accident.

Two people were involved. One lived and one died.

What if rescuing Edgar meant changing everything? What if something had to be sacrificed to save him? Anything could happen.

Adam swallowed hard.

What if I die?

He's worried about the rules now. About sacrifice.

He's still a human.

Keep him on track.

14

*C*lick.

The sound of the closing door filtered into Adam's dream.

He awoke with a gasp.

He'd fallen asleep.

Again.

And he'd had *the* dream.

No. A variation of it.

In this one, Edgar lived. As Adam sank into the ice, he ran away. Ignoring Adam's pleas. Leaving him to die (*the way I left him*) . . .

Adam's heart was racing. He took a deep breath. Shook the thoughts out.

Do. Not. Doubt.

It was light inside. He must have slept through the night. He looked at his clock.

11:57 A.M.

Three more hours.

He swung around. His feet hit the carpet. He reached down for the videocamera.

It was gone.

"Mom? Dad?"

He bolted downstairs. His mom appeared at the bottom landing, looking concerned.

"Where's my videocamera?" Adam asked.

"I gave it to Lianna. She's been over three times this morning. I told her you had a rough night. But she needs to borrow it and I figured — "

Adam heard the front door click.

He ran into the front hallway. Lianna was leaving. *"What are you doing?"* he cried out.

Lianna let go of the door. "Adam! You scared me. I thought you were going to sleep through the whole day. You won't believe this, but Ripley's coming over. He wants your cam-

122

era. When your mom said you were asleep, I figured I'd hide it."

"Look, in three hours he can *have* the stupid camera." *Why is she doing this?* "I don't understand. I thought he wanted to go with me. That was the whole point."

"Does anything about Ripley make sense? Maybe he wants to do it himself and take all the credit."

Adam held out his hand. "Thanks, Lianna, but I can take care of myself."

"He's very persuasive. He'll get it from you."

"Over my dead body."

"That is *such* a bad choice of words."

Ripley wants to go into the past. I want to go into the past. And Lianna's the one with the camera.

Paranoia. Adam tried desperately to fight it back. But he couldn't.

"This has nothing to do with Ripley," Adam blurted out. "*You* want the camera, don't you?"

"Adam, I'm sorry. I can't sit by and let you do this to yourself."

Not now. Now when I'm so close.

"I saved your grandmother's life, Lianna! I saved Jazz's life. I can do for Edgar what I did for them. Even if you don't believe me, *just give me a chance.*"

"You really had me going for a while, Adam. But I've been thinking about this. And I believe something's wrong with you. Something you need to see a doctor about. Your memories are blocked, and somehow looking through a broken camera unblocks them. You're seeing forgotten things, things that really happened — the way a hypnotist would make you see them."

NO!

Adam reached for the camera but Lianna pulled it back. "Trust me on this, Adam," she continued. "I haven't wanted to tell you this, but . . . you won't like what you see."

"Why? What did I do? Have you been lying to me?"

"Don't go there, Adam," Lianna said levelly, backing to the front door. "Stay home."

Lies.

She's been misleading me for four years.

For what?

To make me wonder the rest of my life.

To protect me from the truth.

Adam wasn't going to stand for it any longer. He lunged for the camera.

Ding-dong!

Lianna jumped toward the door and opened it.

Ripley was leaning against the doorjamb, picking his teeth. "So. When's the big time trip?"

He nimbly lifted the videocamera from Lianna's arms.

"NO!" Lianna and Adam yelled.

"Whoa, easy, guys," Ripley handed the camera over to Adam. "I'm not going to eat it."

Adam was stunned. "I thought — don't you want — ?"

"I want to come along. When you go to the lake. Like I said before." He smiled. "Maybe I can meet your friend Edgar."

Adam didn't know who to believe. Or what.

Maybe Lianna was right. Maybe he needed a doctor.

But even if the camera was a fake — even if all it did was unblock his memories — wasn't that enough?

Isn't that all I'm after anyway?

He wasn't sure anymore.

But he did know on thing.

This was between him and Edgar.

No one else.

"Please go home. Both of you." He began crowding Ripley and Lianna out the door.

"Okay, okay, let's go," Ripley said, pulling Lianna onto the porch.

"Get your hands off me!" Lianna shook herself loose and turned to Adam. "Please, you can't do this!"

"That's my decision."

He slammed the door.

Doubts, doubts, doubts.

Patience.

But he questions his sanity.

That may be his salvation.

Do you believe that?

Do you?

15

2:37.

No matter how hard Adam pedaled, Lianna and Ripley were right behind.

"WOOOOO!" Ripley shouted. "This is cool!"

"Knock it off!" Lianna shouted back. "You have no clue! He needs our help. He thinks he brought my grandmother and my dog back from the dead!"

Screaming.

She was revealing Adam's secret to the world.

Focus.

Move.

"Maybe if this works with Edgar," Ripley yelled, "he can bring back Minerva!"

"Who?" Lianna asked.

"My goldfish! She died when I was six!"

A joke. That's what this was to Ripley.

Forget them.

Adam forced his legs to pump. He felt faint. Sick. Split inside between *shouldn't* and *must.*

Must was winning.

It only needed twenty minutes.

The neighborhood houses were giving way to tall pines. Adam swerved up onto the sidewalk, then cut sharply onto the familiar dirt trail.

He gritted his teeth as his bike juddered over exposed roots.

The clearing was empty. Good.

He skidded to a stop near the narrow footpath that led to the lake.

A quick look at the watch. 2:42.

Eighteen minutes.

Adam dropped the bike. He sprinted onto the path, unslinging his backpack.

"OW!"

Lianna.

Don't pay attention. Not enough time.

"Leave me alone, Ripley!"

Adam stopped. He spun around.

Lianna was on the ground and Ripley was huddled over her.

The jerk.

Adam sprinted back into the clearing. He grabbed Ripley's shoulder. "Stop!"

"I'm trying to help!"

Lianna was clutching her ankle. "I think I broke it. Adam, you have to get me to the emergency room."

"Well, I — I — " Adam looked at his watch.

"I'll do it," Ripley volunteered.

"No!" Lianna sprang off the ground and snatched Adam's backpack. Startled, he tripped and fell against a tree.

"Guess the ankle's okay," Ripley said.

Adam clutched his head. "Give it to me, Lianna."

"Adam, look at yourself," Lianna replied. "You're staggering around. You're hysterical. *Something is seriously wrong with you.* I can't let you do this stupid trick. You'll kill yourself."

"Give it to me!"

"Adam, you won't be able to live with the truth!"

Adam lunged for the camera.

Lianna began to run.

"Hey!" Ripley shouted.

He and Adam both took off after Lianna. She raced into the clearing and mounted her bike.

Ripley reached her first. He grabbed hold of Lianna's bike handle with one hand. With the other, he pulled the backpack off her.

"Ripleyyyyyy!" Lianna cried out.

"Take it!" Ripley shoved the backpack into Adam's arms.

He was holding Lianna back. Restraining her.

Ripley.

Adam was stunned. "Thanks."

"Just go before it's too late!"

"NO-O-O-O-O!"

Lianna's voice faded as Adam raced toward the lake.

He glanced at the time.

2:46.

Power switch. On.

Viewfinder. Up.

Adam looked through it.

The image was fuzzy. White. As it cleared, revealing the frozen lake, Adam panned left to right.

There. By the pine grove. Three bulky bodies. Hockey jerseys over down coats.

Edgar.

Even from this distance, he was impossible to miss. Skating around with the puck. Faking left. Right. Taunting and teasing.

The other two were skating after him.

Go to them. Now.

He had to set the camera down. Someplace where no one would see it.

Adam looked around frantically. Behind him stood a gnarled tree, with a fork about three feet off the ground.

He jammed the videocamera into the fork. Pressing his eye to the viewfinder, he focused on the trio.

They were fighting now.

This was the part Adam didn't remember. The part Lianna had told him about. The fight between Adam and Edgar.

The fight that killed my best friend.

He managed to keep his finger on the zoom button, making the image rush closer.

The two kids were in a wrestling hold. Edgar pushed, and they split away from each other. Glaring angrily. Yelling inaudible words.

Adam got a clear look at both of their faces now.

Edgar's.

And Lianna's.

Lianna's?

Adam's younger self was off to the side, looking bewildered. Shouting something that looked like "Stop."

No. This isn't what happened.

This isn't at all what Lianna said.

Young Adam was grabbing Lianna's jersey now, trying to pull her away. Edgar was laughing, shaking his head, skating away with the puck.

With a sudden, angry swipe of her arm, Lianna broke away from Adam's grip.

She skated after Edgar, her hockey stick chest-high.

Adam's younger self was after her, but she'd had a big head start.

She raised the stick.

With a sharp thrust, she brought it down on Edgar's head.

Edgar fell sharply to his knees. He clutched his skull, howling in pain.

Young Adam turned to Lianna in disbelief. She backed away silently, blankly.

Below Edgar, the ice cracked.

He fell into the water, screaming.

GO!

The older Adam ran forward, around the tree. Into the camera's line of sight.

Blip.

Snow crunched under his shoes.

Wind lashed his face.

Edgar was about fifty yards away — floundering, bobbing in the water. Alive, but barely.

Adam — thin, scared, ten-year-old Adam the Wimp — was lying on the ice, right hand locked around Edgar's wrist. Lianna was backing away, slack-mouthed.

As the older Adam ran, his lungs bursting, he remembered the dreams. The images he had buried under guilt and fear and misplaced trust.

It wasn't me. It was Lianna.

"You killed him!" The words burst from his wind-seared lungs.

The young Lianna screamed, "No!"

Adam dived, his own hand outstretched.

He landed hard.

On bare ice.

Solid, snowless ice.

Edgar was gone.

The younger Adam and Lianna, nowhere.

Adam spun around.

Lianna — fourteen-year-old Lianna — was running into the woods, the videocamera tucked under her arm.

We underestimated her.

Sometimes the bad guys win.

16

"**N**O-O-O-O-O-O-O!"

Adam sprinted back across the ice.

He saw Ripley emerge from the woods, racing after Lianna.

As Adam reached the edge of the lake, Ripley tackled Lianna to the ground. The camera tumbled away.

Adam ran for it, but Ripley was there first.

Lianna leaped onto Ripley's back, digging her fingers into his arms. "It's too late, Adam!"

Ripley thrust the camera toward Adam. "Go for it!"

Adam grabbed the camera. For a split second, he caught Lianna's glance.

Desperate. Afraid.

She didn't know he'd already seen it.

"Go!" Ripley repeated. "I've got her!"

Adam ran back onto the ice, digging hard. He'd have to do this on the fly, the way he'd handled Jazz's accident. He lifted the viewfinder awkwardly to his eye.

Edgar wasn't underwater yet. The younger Adam was still on solid ice, pulling hard.

The young Lianna stood frozen. Shocked. Motionless.

Yes. This was in the dream.

But so was —

Crrrrrrrack!

The ice broke for the second time. Adam saw his younger self fall through the crack. Still holding Edgar's hand.

The older Adam ran faster. Crouching, holding the camera with his left hand, he reached with his right.

The outline of his hand was faint. But

there was no mistaking the feel of Edgar's hockey glove.

HOLD HIM!

He pulled. Hard. Edgar's eyes were closed now. He was dead weight.

Dead, *wet* weight.

Adam heard Lianna's voice now. Screaming. She was running away.

The younger Adam was fighting for his own life, gasping for air, flailing his arms.

A sacrifice.

"No!" Adam cried out.

He wanted to reach for his younger self. But he couldn't let go of the camera.

I can't let myself die!

Edgar's hand was growing softer in his. As if it were dematerializing.

DON'T LOSE HIM.

Adam concentrated. The grip tightened.

Out of the corner of his eye, he saw his younger self moving closer, ramming his shoulder into Edgar's side.

Gulping water, turning blue, the younger Adam was trying to shove Edgar out of the hole.

The older Adam jerked backward. Suddenly Edgar was sliding toward him, *upward*, over the jagged lip of ice.

It was going to work.

Just hang on . . . both of you . . .

The older Adam gave a strong yank.

His left foot slid.

Edgar's hand slipped out. His body dropped away.

Adam pitched forward. He opened his mouth in a silent scream.

The camera fell from his eye.

His hands reached out — to nothing.

In a flash of brilliant white, he saw the camera drop.

Through the ice.

Into the past.

Into the lake.

With Edgar.

How could he have lost it?

Perhaps we can bring it back.

No. Some things even we can't do.

17

Gone.

It was all gone.

Into the crack, Adam realized. *It fell into its own image of the past.*

He knew he should scream. Or cry. But he couldn't.

He didn't feel a thing.

Adam surveyed the smooth, unbroken ice. The snowless banks.

His arms were no longer wet. His head no longer ached.

Like it never happened.

As if he'd just awakened from another of his dreams.

Maybe that's all it was. A trick of a disturbed mind. A four-day haze of memories coming unchained. Like Lianna said.

But it was over. And this time he remembered everything.

This time he knew the truth.

Lianna had lied to him. That was why she'd tried to take away the camera. So he couldn't see. So he couldn't know what she'd done.

She killed him.

Maybe.

Without the head injury, Edgar might have survived. He might have been conscious longer. He might have been able to hold tighter. To respond to Adam's help.

What was the difference now?

Edgar had died.

Twice.

Adam realized that through all the deception, Lianna had been right about one other thing.

He couldn't take it.

He began to shake.

A moan welled up from somewhere deep inside him, buried under four years of grief. It exploded from his mouth. Then another, and another.

No one responded. Lianna and Ripley were probably halfway across town by now.

He sat there until he couldn't moan anymore. Until he could barely feel.

Later — how long? Five minutes? Two hours? — Adam pulled up in front of Ripley's house.

To thank him.

To let him know how much Adam had misjudged him.

But also to ask his advice. Eventually Adam would have to confront Lianna. One-on-one. And Ripley would know how to do it.

He rang the doorbell once. Twice.

Finally he heard a commotion inside.

The door flew open. "Heyyyyy, what's up?" called a familiar voice.

Adam's throat locked up. He tried to speak, but no sound would come out.

"Adam? Did something happen?"

Adam swallowed hard and blinked.

Then he looked up at his friend's face.

Edgar.

I didn't think he could.

A little faith is all it takes.
Sometimes.

18

The furniture. The Persian rug. The grandfather clock.

It was all back.

Edgar's stuff.

Edgar's house.

"Uh, Earth to Adam," Edgar said.

"Where's Ripley?" Adam asked.

"Ripley who?"

"You don't — he didn't — but Lianna *killed* you."

Edgar gave him a strange look, then called

151

over his shoulder, "Hey, did you happen to kill me?"

Lianna walked in from the kitchen, munching on a Ring-Ding. She was dressed in a hockey jersey. "Don't tempt me."

Adam was reeling.

Ripley's family never moved here.

Because Edgar lived on.

And so did Lianna's lie.

"Adam?" Edgar asked. "Are you all right?"

Adam shook his head. "No. I'm not. *Nothing* is. Edgar, remember that accident four years ago? On the ice? You — you were supposed to die that day!"

Stop. His death never happened, Adam.

"Is this some kind of weird joke?" Edgar asked.

"Do you remember what happened?" Adam struggled to keep his voice calm.

"You *know* I don't," Edgar replied. "I was wiped out, just like you. Traumatic stress, whatever they call it."

Adam faced Lianna. "What did you tell him? You saved me *and* him? You're twice a hero?"

Lianna groaned. "God, you're not bringing

that up again, are you? Okay, you want to take credit for it? Fine."

"It's a lie," Adam said. "You were the one fighting with Edgar. You hit him with a hockey stick."

Lianna's face turned pale. "Where did you hear that crazy idea — ?"

"Then, when we fell through, you just stood there and watched. You didn't get help. After a while you started screaming — someone must have heard it. *That's* how we were saved. How convenient for you that Edgar and I didn't remember."

"No one was there, Adam. No one could have seen any of that!"

"I was there, Lianna. I saw."

"Oh. Right." Lianna let out a strange, nervous laugh. She began backing up toward Edgar's door. "This is like some kind of buried memory that came back in one of your dreams? This is silly, Adam. I'm hurt."

Edgar looked from Adam to Lianna. "Where are you going?"

"*He's* the one lying, Edgar!" Lianna swallowed hard. Her eyes darted. "You have no proof, Adam."

"Do *you*?"

"I will not stand here and be insulted!" With that, she ran out of the house.

Adam fought the impulse to chase her.

Let her go. For now.

"Do you really remember?" Edgar asked, his face full of doubt.

Adam nodded. "We have a lot to talk about."

Below them, the front door slammed. Edgar sank onto the bed, lost in thought. Confused.

Maybe it's best to just leave it alone, Adam thought.

Let it die.

The squeal of tires made Adam jump.

He and Edgar ran to the window.

The first thing Adam saw was a hockey jersey.

Lianna's.

She was lying on the road, facedown.

A car had skidded to a stop, diagonally across the road.

A green Volvo.

Lianna's grandmother was pushing the driver's door open, screaming.

"Oh my god," Adam murmured.

Edgar was already out the door. "Let's help her!"

Adam followed.

It was the least he could do.

WATCHERS
Case File: 6791

Name: Adam Sarno

Age: 14

First contact: 54.35.20

Acceptance: YES

Marion Ettlinger

ABOUT THE AUTHOR

Peter Lerangis is the author of more than one hundred books, including two Young Adult thrillers, *The Yearbook* and *Driver's Dead*. He was once a stage actor, which often allowed him to travel into the past. He still enjoys doing it as an author, although he misses the costumes. Mr. Lerangis lives in New York City with his wife, Tina deVaron, and his two sons, Nick and Joe.